DEMAIN PU

Short Sharp Shocks!

Book 0: Dirty Paws - Dean M. Drinkel
Book 1: Patient K - Barbie Wilde
Book 2: The Stranger & The Ribbon – Tim Dry
Book 3: Asylum Of Shadows – Stephanie Ellis
Book 4: Monster Beach – Ritchie Valentine Smith
Book 5: Beasties & Other Stories – Martin Richmond
Book 6: Every Moon Atrocious – Emile-Louis Tomas Jouvet
Book 7: A Monster Met – Liz Tuckwell
Book 8: The Intruders & Other Stories – Jason D. Brawn
Book 9: The Other – David Youngquist
Book 10: Symphony Of Blood – Leah Crowley
Book 11: Shattered – Anthony Watson
Book 12: The Devil's Portion – Benedict J. Jones
Book 13: Cinders Of A Blind Man Who Could See – Kev Harrison
Book 14: Dulce Et Decorum Est – Dan Howarth
Book 15: Blood, Bears & Dolls – Allison Weir
Book 16: The Forest Is Hungry – Chris Stanley
Book 17: The Town That Feared Dusk – Calvin Demmer
Book 18: Night Of The Rider – Alyson Faye
Book 19: Isidora's Pawn – Erik Hofstatter
Book 20: Plain – D.T. Griffith
Book 21: Supermassive Black Mass – Matthew Davis
Book 22: Whispers Of The Sea (& Other Stories) – L. R. Bonehill
Book 23: Magic – Eric Nash
Book 24: The Plague – R.J. Meldrum
Book 25: Candy Corn – Kevin M. Folliard
Book 26: The Elixir – Lee Allen Howard
Book 27: Breaking The Habit – Yolanda Sfetsos
Book 28: Forfeit Tissue – C. C. Adams

Book 29: Crown Of Thorns – Trevor Kennedy
Book 30: The Encampment / Blood Memory – Zachary Ashford
Book 31: Dreams Of Lake Drukka / Exhumation – Mike Thorn
Book 32: Apples / Snail Trails – Russell Smeaton
Book 33: An Invitation To Darkness – Hailey Piper
Book 34: The Necessary Evils & Sick Girl – Dan Weatherer
Book 35: The Couvade – Joe Koch
Book 36: The Camp Creeper & Other Stories – Dave Jeffery
Book 37: Flaying Sins – Ian Woodhead
Book 38: Hearts & Bones – Theresa Derwin
Book 39: The Unbeliever & The Intruder – Morgan K. Tanner
Book 40: The Coffin Walk – Richard Farren Barber
Book 41: The Straitjacket In The Woods – Kitty R. Kane
Book 42: Heart Of Stone – M. Brandon Robbins
Book 43: Bits – R.A. Busby
Book 44: Last Meal In Osaka & Other Stories – Gary Buller
Book 45: The One That Knows No Fear – Steve Stred
Book 46: The Birthday Girl & Other Stories – Christopher Beck
Book 47: Crowded House & Other Stories - S.J. Budd
Book 48: Hand To Mouth – Deborah Sheldon
Book 49: Moonlight Gunshot Mallet Flame / A Little Death – Alicia Hilton
Book 50: Dark Corners - David Charlesworth

Murder! Mystery! Mayhem!

Maggie Of My Heart – Alyson Faye
The Funeral Birds – Paula R.C. Readman
Cursed – Paul M. Feeney
The Bone Factory – Yolanda Sfetsos

Garland Cove – Deborah Sheldon
Death In The Dugout – Bruce Harris

Beats! Ballads! Blank Verse!

Book 1: Echoes From An Expired Earth – Allen Ashley
Book 2: Grave Goods – Cardinal Cox
Book 3: From Long Ago – Paul Woodward
Book 4: Laws Of Discord – William Clunie
Book 5: Fanged Dandelion – Eric LaRocca

Weird! Wonderful! Other Worlds

Book 1: The Raven King – Liz Tuckwell
Book 2: The Wired City – Yolanda Sfetsos

Horror Novels & Novellas

House Of Wrax – Raven Dane
And Blood Did Fall – Chad A. Clark
The Fallen – Anthony Watson
The Underclass – Dan Weatherer
Cheslyn Myre – Dan Weatherer
Greenbeard – John Travis
Tower Of Raven – Kevin M. Folliard
Welcome Home Natalie – Reyna Young
Little Bird – TR Hitchman
Society Place – Andrew David Barker
Axe – Terry Grimwood
Wicked Blood – E.C. Hanson
The Again-Walkers – Deborah Sheldon
Between The Teeth Of Charon – Grant Longstaff
One Ampoule Of Terror – Carrie Weston

Science Fiction Novels & Novellas

Odyssey Of The Black Turtle – Paul Woodward
Sons Of Sol – Kevin R. McNally

The 'A QUIET APOCALYPSE' Series
A Quiet Apocalypse – Dave Jeffery
Cathedral (A Quiet Apocalypse Book 2) – Dave Jeffery
The Samaritan (A Quiet Apocalypse Book 3) – Dave Jeffery
A Silent Dystopia (Stories Of A Quiet Apocalypse) – Edited by D.T. Griffith

General Fiction
Joe – Terry Grimwood
Finding Jericho – Dave Jeffery

Science Fiction Collections
Vistas – Chris Kelso

Horror Fiction Collections
Distant Frequencies – Frank Duffy
Where We Live – Tim Cooke
Night Voices – Paul Edwards & Frank Duffy
The Singing Sands & Other Stories – Rudolf Kremers

Anthologies
The Darkest Battlefield – Tales Of WW1/Horror

ONE AMPOULE OF TERROR

BY
CARRIE WESTON

© Demain 2022

COPYRIGHT INFORMATION

Entire contents copyright © 2022 Carrie Weston / Demain Publishing

Cover © 2022 Adrian Baldwin
Cover Art © 2022 Roberto Segate
Cover Model - Tia
First Published 2022

All rights reserved. No part of this publication may be reproduced, stored or transmitted in any form or by any means, electronic, mechanical, photocopying, recording, scanning or otherwise without written permission from the publisher. It is illegal to copy this book, post it to a website or distribute it by any other means without permission.

What follows is entirely a work of fiction. The names, characters and incidents portrayed in it are the work of the author's imagination. Any resemblance to actual persons, living or dead, events or localities is entirely co-incidental.

Carrie Weston asserts the moral right to be identified as the author of this work in its totality.

Designations used by companies to distinguish their products are often claimed as trademarks. All brand names and product names used in this book and on its cover are trade names, service marks, trademarks and registered trademarks of their respective owners. The publishers and the book are not associated with any product or vendor mentioned in this book. None of the companies within the book have endorsed the book.

For further information, please visit:
WEB: www.demainpublishing.com
TWITTER: @DemainPubUk
FACEBOOK: Demain Publishing
INSTAGRAM: demainpublishing

For my father, the Helsing in my life and my mother—whose friendship means as much as Peaches does to Sally Ann.

CONTENTS

ONE AMPOULE OF TERROR   **11**
BIOGRAPHY & THANKS   **53**
DEMAIN PUBLISHING   **55**

ONE AMPOULE OF TERROR

PART 1
Gilbert Townsworth exited a large timber crate studded with wrought iron nails. He pulled a pristine white handkerchief from the inner pocket of his speckled suit jacket and wiped at the attached drill upgrade in place of his prosthetic hand. He tilted his head, his tongue tracing his thick bottom lip, as he watched the slick carnage drip from his prosthetic and into the expendable fabric. The stark crimson set his heart aglow; he could practically taste the gelatinous terror pouring from the crate's unsealed entrance. It was a shame there was no room for a lamp in there so that he could admire his masterpiece but so it goes. He smiled his delight, in what his daughter called a 'mouth-splitting grin', stretching high from cheek to cheek. The grittiest parts the handkerchief bore were mesmerising against its stark white, glaring in protest. Beguiling him into a willing slave with the compulsion to sniff at its gouged contents.

Death had always smelled good to him. An intoxicating scent of iron, magnesium, and terror. He lived to bottle that aroma, and one day, he would.

Carefully folding the sodden material, he walked with slow steps back to the open crate. His cane lay propped against it, its swollen globe head hidden by the shadow of his aristocratic top hat unceremoniously dumped atop. A deep throaty moan gurgled from the timber crate; its volume hardly heard through the thick planks. But still, Gilbert could feel the delicious vibration of every cell within his circulatory system as his mind elevated, reaching a crescendo of numbness and his body purred to life. *This was the job of wet dreams*, he thought, his tongue sliding to moisten his plumping lower lip. He shivered in ecstasy at the deep burn pulsating in his swollen gums, holding back a moan of wanting as he relieved his cane of the top hat and placed it atop of his hairless, pale scalp.

Glaring down at the globe of his cane, a sharp smile punctuating his bulbous gums, he thumbed the catch to release a mechanism of clockwork parts that twirled and swirled like a mist as they formulated an intricate crystal ball. From within it grew soft thick lashes of the purest black, snaking deep blue eyes rimmed with stardust. The lightly blushed hue of sickly skin came next before he could gaze upon wanton lips of the deepest colour of blood. Long, satin black hair cascaded from beneath a delicate lace-trimmed bonnet. Gilbert stared at his daughter in adoration. "Good tidings, Father," his child purred, smiling with bright white teeth. "What news have you for me? Is it my birthday gift? Could it be; is it ready?" The girl's eyes popped wide in her small-framed face through the midst of the seeing mechanism.

"Oh, you do so rush an old man," he croaked, his throat thick with saliva. "I have not yet harvested your gift, my child. But soon, soon you shall have it." He smiled, a twitch of his elongated earlobes betraying the stress that heated his swollen red gums. "Until then, daughter, I have a token from the late Mr. Gibbs." He cupped the sodden handkerchief and lifted it to the mechanism's whirling globe. "Mittere," he ordered, and it suddenly disappeared from his palm to reappear inside the globe before being transported into the little girl's twitching hand.

As he had, his child echoed his enthusiasm and delicately sniffed at the pulpy material, sighing deeply before falling back in a halo of hair upon her black-suited bed. The mechanism began to whirl, its inner smoke consuming the globe and fading his beloved child from sight.

Gilbert stroked the cane's bulbous crystal adoringly before thrusting the tip of his staff deep into the earth where it stood century as he lifted the crate's timber seal with unimaginable strength. He whispered "Sigillum," to his cane, watching as the globe shone with a smoky carnelian light and one by one, the nails sought their holes, grinding through the timber as if hammered there. He chuckled wetly. "Farewell, Mr. Gibbs." He smiled, content in the knowledge that before sunrise, the crate would be manhandled onto a docked steamship and sent on its way. The day the man's remains were uncovered they would be far away in a country foreign to his own. Far enough away for suspicions to be cast from his association with the timber crate. For who would un-nail a box sent from a Lord at a mere shipping doc? Especially when said Lord always had his own servants prepare his crates for shipping. That the Lord never showed his face, nor was ever seen was beyond suspicion, for he would pay handsomely for his lesser's silence. Even if they discovered something unseemly. That, or they would mysteriously disappear. He chuckled sardonically.

Gilbert weaved his way through the timber crates stacking the docking yards inner holding shed, admiring his handiwork on the stamps of those ready to ship from the elusive Lord. Oh, how he loved to play with the tiny minds of men. He walked faster with the aid of his cane, supplicating that the globe mechanism would not dial with the tone of the Council who consistently stalked his movements. He eyed the cane serendipitously. Some people would think him weak for using such an implement, but his strength had nothing to do with the defect boring into his left leg. No, that was purely Athos's fault. Athos, whose pretty little daughter Sally Ann was his next unsuspecting test subject.

PART 2

Sally Ann usually sat with her back to the walled garden, for its fortunate position meant she could keep watch on the comings and goings of the gothic manor's staff, whilst seeing one of her more favoured features of the building, a statue carved of red stone. Its little features were hard to see from the semi-circular lawn where she played, but she knew them by heart, knew the vivid indents of barred teeth and the pointed ears of a guarding canine wrapped up in the vision of a gargoyle that loomed over the wooden entrance doors spilling out over the foreboding sight of her governess, who trudged a crunching path of chalked stones beneath her heavily heeled boots. She knew the woman was coming for her, her timing was always impeccable prompt when it came to the evening dining, probably so she could usher her to her chamber not half an hour hence and be rid of the nuisance that she dubbed her.

Sally Ann turned back to her toys, continuing their much-awaited picnic. Ignoring the ever-increasing volume of crunching stones heading her way. She had always preferred playing outside in the warm glow of the sun that sat there like a giant sunflower bowing gracefully over her. She poured yet another cup of imaginary tea, for one of her many toys joining her tea party, on the back lawn beneath the lace parasol her papa brought her back from one of his increasing visits to the city for business he would never talk about with her, for she need not worry her little head about adult tidings. For the ventures of men were no place for little girls. Sally Ann huffed, placing the freshly poured tea before Sally doll junior. Sat cross legged next to her was Mary and her lamb then Teddy Brown and her most favoured of them all, Peaches.

Peaches was a mohair bear with a round little tummy in which nestled a vaseline glass heart that glowed the warmest of yellows even in the night. She had a big peach bow wrapped around its neck still from where her papa had tied it as he gifted it to her in her seventh year. Sally Ann handed Peaches the last cup of tea before tending to herself, her eyes never leaving its beady ones.

"I love you, Peaches," she crooned, slipping forwards to pull the bear into her warm embrace. "Now don't you ever leave me, you hear? No running off. Not even to get the sugared almonds off of that funny old man." She stared hard at the bear, tilting her head to the side, the pale strings of her bonnet tickling as she pretended to listen. "You know very well which man I speak of." Pausing again to raise an eyebrow at her motionless bear, she concluded, "The one who has been walking the property's boundaries; that very same one. He is a stranger and that's not safe." She pulled the soft wool bear into a squished embrace, delighting in its little glass heart glowing brighter in the shadow of their bodies. "I wouldn't know what to do if I lost you." Her voice quaked and a single tear ran down her rosy cheek. "You're my everything. My world." That's what Papa had always said to her every evening when he was home and kissed her before bed. But Papa wasn't here right now. He had gone to chase the Almond Man away the evening prior and had not yet returned. Now she was stuck with Mrs. Stephens, her smelly old governess, who didn't think she noticed the gin bottle she kept strapped in her skirts. Undoubtedly, her papa had yet to discover this or the woman would already have been thrown out. Sally Ann should have informed him of such goings-on, but truly she did not want to jeopardise the freedom she had when her governess had been crooking her elbow. The way she figured it Papa had always said a lady should mind her own business, so she had, choosing to set her tea party up on the lawn in the fresh afternoon air; it was good for her lungs.

  She played with her china tea set, the one with gold painted rabbits that hopped around the rim playfully and imagined cakes of all grandeur—from can-baked currant cakes with sweet smelling spices to glazed fruit squares. She separated out the imaginary confectionary and cut pieces off for her fluffy friends and dolls until the light began to wane and her governess, who stopped to sneak a little liquor behind a potted tree, decided to retrieve her from her playthings. Sally Ann pulled away in discord when the woman wrenched her by the arm, flinging herself to the chequered blanket strewn on the soft summer grass, scrabbling for Peaches before the wretched woman could grasp hold of her again.

  "Get up this instant," her blotchy, red-faced governess cried, all too aware that her papa had promised to return before sunset. "Miss Sally, young ladies do not scrabble about the floor." She bent down, her multitude of skirts bunching as she clawed at the little girl's wrist, tightening her hold. "Come along now," she slurred, wrenching her back toward the manor again.

More than happy that she had successfully rescued Peaches from being suffocated inside of the blanket when the servants cleared up her toys, Sally Ann happily complied, although the crushing grip on her wrist brought tears to her eyes.

"—elp."

"Oh, Miss Sally, what a fuss you make," scolded the governess.

"I—That—" A sharp lurch ceased her stuttered response before she could clarify her non-involvement.

An almighty thud had the governess freezing in her tracks, her attention turning towards the boarding wood of the property as she tried to comprehend the cry of a rasping baritone that had the very leaves on the summer trees shivering their discomfort, through her drunken stupor.

"—elp!" came the groan again.

"Should we not call the butler? Is that not what Papa would wish?" Sally Ann voiced softly.

Her governess's face flushed a deep puce. Her grip on the girl tightened in warning, imprinting a red glow where her fingertips had dug in before she released her. Sally Ann hugged her bear to her chest as the marks on her arm receded, ignoring her governesses, who commanded: "The hour is late. You must wash for dinner. Return to the manor while I investigate that insufferable racket."

Sally Ann primped her apron, puffed out her cheeks, and stamped one white little slippered foot as she watched the older woman heave her heavy skirts and stalk determinedly across the lawn, her heavy footfalls imprinting the spongy grass as she stormed into the sentry of trees before disappearing from sight. She waited, but by the third tap of her slipper upon the lush grass, her heart was racing like a horse on a racetrack, only to aggrandize the lament of her governess's clamour.

With a deeply embedded instinct to uncover falsehoods and mysteries, Sally Ann's impatience exploded in a stampede of footfalls as she sped toward the calamity. She could not help but spare a distracted smile down at the snowdrops, unable to slow her ascent to show Peaches. She passed the overgrown holly bush with a fleeting thought that her papa, having told her never to venture further, would have been disappointed in her blatant display of disrespect. But regardless, she was spurred on by the mystery as she raced through the opening of dense fir trees, limbs clawing at her like the hands of an aggrieved parent desperately trying to restrain their infant.

But Sally Ann heeded no warning; instead, she delved headlong into the midst of calamity, appearing behind a girthy gentleman pressed intimately against a woman, she deduced from her skirts, was her governess.

Wet sucking sounds smacked around in the veil of branches and Sally Ann's cheeks heated. She had not meant to intrude on a lovers' affair, nor had she, in all her years, known that a gentleman courted her governess. She tried to back away but in her embarrassed haste, her foot stamped down onto a dried twig and the snap of it echoed around the small clearing. A low growl rumbled through the trees, and the furs shook pine leaves free in defence, raining daggers.

Sally Ann's heart hammered like a casket being sealed for burial as the man turned predatorial eyes on her; her every motion was tracked with a twitch of his sallow bald head. Her breath imprisoned itself in her lungs as behind the man she barely dared to look upon, her governess slumped down the tree. In her wake, blood snagged fabric lay a trail to her body as she pooled to the hard ground in a boneless effect, her head lolling heavily to one side, a thin red necklace budding crimson beads which spilled down her dress. Head spinning with lack of oxygen, Sally Ann trembled, terror opening a stain in her mind lucid with the apprehension of horrors that he would bequeath because of her intrusion upon what she could only guess was a lovers' quarrel.

Before her, the man advanced, his shimmering silver eyes snapping to hers, jailing them within his hypnotic gaze. His masochistic smile split his face fiercely from ear to ear, and Sally Ann felt her lips curl in repulsion as she sucked in a deep breath. The man's eyes sparkled in the darkness, all the while watching her swirling irises, and he slowly retracted two large crimson-soaked fangs, his tongue whipping at the sharpened points to catch the last of his sustenance as they returned to their sheathing of grotesquely swollen gums.

Sally Ann screamed, ending his theatrical crescendo, as his prosthetic claw attachment shot out to anchor her to his side. The blood inside her exploded like a volcano and her head began to spin, falling sideways, her body collapsing, a searing pain jolting her arm from its socket. Her eyes fell to stare upon those of Ruby's, her governess, who glared back through snowy sightless eyes, her pallor as dull a grey as any common rock, a trickle of her life's blood running down the ripped collar of her uniform now speckled with tears. Then all was black. No smells, no pain, and no horror; only the emptiness that nothingness provided.

***

Gilbert Townsworth had made sure to be very quiet when stealthily wrapping the child in his suit jacket. The girl merely appeared unwell with her pale complexion as he cradled her in his arms, his cane resting upon her limp body. He hadn't planned on the nosy governess coming to find out what the ruckus was but he had enjoyed the aged, pungent variant that was her blended heritage and the last meal she ate. Gilbert hobbled through the woody outcrop of spruces, pines, and oaks at a speed uncanny to any human, and incomprehensible for their brain's navigational senses. He slowed only as his black pointed shoes bit into the crunching grit of the neighbouring town's uneven cobbled road. A horse and cart rumbled by, and the man atop its worn seat nodded a friendly acknowledgment; while his bay horse whinnied to its master a warning of distrust. Its ears flicking back and forth in alarm, upper lip curled to expose its tombstone teeth as it held its tail to its hindquarters and recoiled into the cart before its senseless master whipped it to a canter. The cart's wheels kicked up stones, raining them in its wake.

Shaking his head at the foolish man, his satin top hat slipping slightly over one cauliflower ear, Gilbert pressed on—this time at a pace others could clearly see, for it would not do to cast their eyes on blurry shadows in the evening light. Frightened men were a challenge to work his operations around, especially when they called notice to the constables who policed the town he currently resided near.

Hobbling along with the girl wrapped snug, but securely in his arms, her intoxicating scent was enough to have his heart beating a staccato against his ribs. His shirt bellowed from his suit trousers pooling a train beneath the child whose pallor challenged the fall of freshly lain snow. He barely glanced at the girl out here in the open, for fear his hope would shatter upon the commencement of his ministrations. But she could very well be the one. And for her to be the kin of the sworn enemy of his kind just added the final pinch of tantalising RH-null, the rarest and most decadent of all the lifeblood, as a topper. His tongue snaked out to sweep his lips; his mouth was still uncomfortably full. He was getting old now and his fangs took longer to retract than that of a youngling, hence his subtle grimace as he returned the greetings of towns-people he cared not to remember his presence.

His steps slowed as pavements framed either side of the cobbled street he wished he had the patience to avoid travelling through. But alas, it would have taken him considerable effort, and the expense of valuable time, to skirt the small town just budding with evening life. Shops of convenience and administrations lined the road. Ads, and pictures displayed in the windows. Gilbert did not care. But, from time to time, it became advantageous for him to appear mulling over their prospects, avoiding the considerable questions he knew concerned citizens would impart. His aiding cane rocked on top of the child as she breathed through her fainting hysteria. He had unknowingly begun the terror that would make his daughter's elixir just by the noisiness of a stupid governess. He chuckled to himself as he avoided the majority of people. All except one.

"Oh, my goodness!" wailed a woman, her bustle and bonnet the colour of freshly fallen snow. She stood before him, blocking his way, as was her intent. "What happened? It is Miss Sally Ann, is it not?" She looked at him expectantly and he grimaced like a cat around its kill. "So far from home, poor thing; is she sick?" She gazed empathic blue eyes into his, her parlour wilting slightly.

Gilbert sucked in his lips, his fangs scraping down them, and replied, "Taking her to Doctor Ernest. Little Miss had a little fall." His words were slurred and slow, but they seemed to pacify the woman who moved from his way, bestowing her best wishes in a sickeningly sweet tone before calling to a lady across the way and pursuing her through a confectionery's door.

Gilbert hobbled faster; the doctor's home was not far down this lane and it wouldn't do to attract the attention of any other lady socialite obsessed with the town's talk this evening. The night was drawing in. There were thick waterlogged clouds, but they had yet to burst the confines of atmospheric oppressions and rain tears down upon the earth, sending the nosy humans scattering to their homes and the comfort of glowing fires while he—he would have some fun.

***

Sally Ann's arm burnt; the deep throb swelling her shoulder joint was strangled in the lace of her speckled dress. Moaning, she took a shaky breath, rubbing at her head which thumped like a kettle drum in time with her heart.

She clenched her right fist, checking for Peaches' fluffy paw and jerking awake the second she felt its emptiness. It was dark, night maybe. She began to move, but her shoulder protested the moment it slid from its resting place against a wall of roughened wood. She leaned back, squinting hard into the black depths of her surroundings, scanning for Peaches' glowing heart. The cool air scented with salt whistled through the slatted boards of a makeshift door.

Two small pinpricks of light caught her attention. She watched them, baring her teeth in pain as the molten silver of eyes much like that of a cat studied her back. Her heart started to thrum and a shiver swept like the touch of a ghost down her spine, raising the tiny hairs on her neck to stand like barbed wire. The closer it came, the fuzzier her thoughts became—the images of something awful, terrifying, horrific coming to be from her memory.

First came the tread of uneven feet upon a ringing surface, echoing its malevolence.

Second, the stifled breath of over-enthusiastic excitement mixed with a deep yearning passion forbidden to surface in one's presence.

Third, remembrance, as images of the past afternoon flooded her mind. She screamed. Flashing eyes of silver power, fangs so sharp they struck and sparked a fountain of crimson belonging to her governess, whose body lay dead like a shell on the shore, left for spectators to wonder at. "Dear God," she began to pray but then he was before her, the monster in her mind, alive, real, and licking his plump lips around grotesquely swollen gums.

***

Gilbert stalked forwards, the slow scrape of his knobbed leg's foot sliding eerily behind him. He had left his top hat and cane outside the wooden board seal of the shipping container that housed his unsuccessful experiment specimens.

"Looking for something?" he asked with a sharp smile, his words hissing slightly.

"Who are you?" Her shrill little voice hit the air and Gilbert almost purred at the satisfaction their tremoring notes held. He shivered, his eyes aglow with stardust that cast an ethereal glow in the thick darkness of suffocating gloom.

He listened to the shallow breathing of his prey as it fluttered like a hummingbird trapped in a cage. He stepped closer, stumbling over a lump he did not care to see, but by the hitch of breath the child took, he could not ignore the thing.

As it turned out, his arthritic gnarled hands clawed the toy, although he did not consider a teddy bear with a glowing centre much of a toy for the daughter of his arch-nemesis. Asoth was getting old if this was all he could gift his daughter to keep her safe. Although he had passed his prime an age ago and as his only heir was female, he would have to take on an apprentice to covert his vampiric work, leaving this luscious specimen full of estrogen ripe for the plucking. He cackled, spittle flying from his mouth in fat globs of crimson rain. His tongue snaked out to catch the few specks that sprayed onto his lips, savouring their layers of fruity sweetness with a lower accent of musk.

"I am your demise, child." He stared down at the girl's watering eyes, her shaking body, and the twitching tap of one pointed toe.

It had been with pure sadistic delight that he had slipped the supple soles of tenderised suede, flecked with the most delicious aroma that punctuated the pure white of each painted toe, from the sickly porcelain feet of the girl. Gilbert licked his lips with the thought of the smooth slick vintage that pulsed through those swollen veins to her toes. Oh, how his daughter had preened at the sight of those beautifully blood glittered slippers. The pure delight they brought her demonic heart was a visible treat as her star-dust eyes sparked like a newly exploded star.

The last time he had seen her eyes spark like that had been the day he proposed to gift her something no other vampiress had. Something more precious than the silks and jewels that had adorned her every undead dream. He had spoiled her, he knew, but to what end would a loving parent not go? So naturally, he had started up the mechanism on his cane, watching it whirl and glow as his daughter's beautiful eyes came into view and he passed the precious gift through the globe to her twitching, waiting palms. That was when he promised her her birthday gift. Promised it her before the week's end.

***

Sally Ann's shoulder throbbed as tears tracked rivers down her pale skin. Her body shook, goosebumps consuming her complexion, the cold steel bite stealing the feeling from her naked toes. The maniac stood in front of her, eyes eerily aglow as he lifted Peaches to his stout nose and sniffed long and hard, making her stomach churn at the race of her beating heart.

Oh, Peaches, I'm so scared! I want Papa! I want to go home! I just want to go home! she thought, sniffling slightly.

The man smiled, stretching his thick lips back from bloody gums as her eyes tracked his every movement as a glint of white slid from his mouth an upside-down pike. Another, on the opposite side, slid out like the tusk of a young walrus and even the warmth trickling from her bowels couldn't defrost the terror freezing her heart as it thumped at her breast, rattling at the bars of her lungs for freedom.

"Please, sir, let me go. Please," she begged through blurry stinging tears, fisting her torn and speckled skirts as she trembled.

The monster before her tilted his head to one side, his eyes wide and sparkling—one hand holding Peaches, who wore the abrasions of time from her last tea party to this maniac's abduction. A guillotine-like attachment stood in place of the man's arm, shimmering with the glint of his wicked eyes. He winked, the unnatural grin pulling tight around swollen gums baring the two large fangs, dripping with the blood from their puncture.

"P-please—"

***

Gilbert chuckled, a wet sound bubbling from his lungs. He didn't have long left in this world. Not because of his sickness—he had coped with that irritant since his change into immortality. No, he didn't have long for this world as Athos would catch up with him and finish what he started. But not before he took his daughter apart piece by juicy piece.

"Let's play a little game shall we, my sweet?" he hissed, clicking the prosthetic guillotine attachment on his arm. The harsh swish-snick-slash of its blade sounded as he tested its bite. The girl trembled and his prominent veins filled with the immortal elixir of reproduction venom from the time his sire created him bubbled and throbbed through his every limb. *This is going to be delicious*, he thought as a pool of wet liquid seeped from the child's bowels.

With a chuckle, Gilbert shook the toy bear, gaining her attention as he pouted, a more difficult feat with his fangs exposed, but he managed just fine, snapping his guillotine with a snick at the bottom of Peaches' paw, severing it clean off. Moving the blade to his teeth, he licked at the stuffing snatched on its edge with the scream of the child as his backing symphony.

"Oh, what a pity, poor... Peaches, was it?" He cocked his head and grinned. "It seems she is missing something."

The girl froze, her heart beating so hard he was surprised she didn't erupt with burst blood vessels. "Well then, what shall we do?" he cooed, scenting the fear in the air like a thick sweet syrup. Oh, he was brewing her terror nicely. But would she be the one? Could he wrench her terror enough for her body to create the first essence of ambrosia? He lurched closer and the child's eyes stretched wide, her mouth falling open to scream, but—

Swish!
Squelch!

Crunch!

***

Sally Ann didn't usually dream. It wasn't in her character to worry about anything. After all, if any dispute arose, it was her papa who attended to it and if it was a product of her fault, then her governess would carry the reprimand.

Never before had she seen someone die, let alone get murdered. That was enough to haunt her fainting spell and keep her from wanting to wake anytime soon. But for the shocking pressure that burnt agony like sunstroke up through her body. Her eyes blinked, suffering sunspots of pain as she tried to focus, a nauseating tremor flooding her throat as all at once she heaved the contents of her stomach, wrenching her agonising shoulder and releasing a guttural roar.

"Ah, good morning," purred the orchestrator of her nightmares, the very devil himself. Sally Ann didn't dare look at him. She didn't dare look at herself either, for the agony searing her foot had a sickly sweat coursing from her brow and a bone-deep shudder rattling her small frame. But when she saw the soft welcoming glow of Peaches not far from where she had collapsed, she wrenched herself forwards to snatch up the bear, cradling her close, her head buried in its fur. But at the deep chuckling of the maniac, Sally Ann's breath caught. She peered from around Peaches, her sodden hair clinging to her face as she dry swallowed.

Her eyes first hit the man's as he moved to lower the dripping pail he had shocked her awake with, the iron bars forging it together glinting in his eerie eyes. His smile was no longer the one that reached each crescent of cheekbone—it was firm in its calculating indecision as his ethereal gaze landed on hers. A single jolt of his head had her instantly obeying his speechless command as her eyes rolled south and her heart picked up speed once again. Her breath exploded from her lungs in one petrified burst, and she pitched to one side, heaving thick green bile as, from the corner of her eye, she saw the maniac's smile slide back into place.

"Oh, my dear, you make this so easy, so... delectable."

That was the moment that Sally Ann knew she would never escape the heinous mad man. Never again see her papa. Never be free; and neither would Peaches, she resigned, staring at the fluffy bear with a dulling glow from its heart highlighting its plumply stuffed leg impaled with industrial staples. Swinging from the toy's staples was the bloody appendage of its mistress. Sally Ann leaned sideways, wrenching her shoulder, and what was left of her crimson stunted foot and heaved. Spittle, bile, and salty tears pooled her horror as her ears rung and head throbbed, barely deciphering the yelling disturbance outside of her prison.

***

"Mr. Townsworth, I won't ask again!" a woman's voice hollered.

Gilbert rolled his eyes, their glow alighting the sickened child. *Near, she is near*, he thought, settling Peaches to sit before the girl and hobbling his way to the makeshift door, stealthily squeezing through.

"There's no point in concealment, Mr. Townsworth. I know of your unethical experiments, as does the Council. I'm just here to serve your warning." The short stump of a woman blared from her entrance amid several large, packed crates. She always did appear at the crux of a precipice, extending the anticipation of a potential possible results. It made him wish he could sink his teeth into her. If he was a few years younger, he would doubt her abilities to stop him. But after having come up against Mistress Beatrice not far off a year ago, he knew not to underestimate her; after all, his own sire had revered her, and she had orchestrated his deployment away from the Council's scientific investigation unit. Besides he doubted they could penetrate the thick hide she sported. Gilbert straightened, his eyes flaring as he forced himself to tilt his head.

"Mistress," he acknowledged, turning to gather his propped cane and top hat. "What can I do for you?"

The stout woman harrumphed, stalked past him with her regal cane embellished to appear the height of a sceptre, and threw aside the makeshift wooden door with one well-aimed strike of her cane's glowing mechanism. Her fangs instantly materialised with the sweet scent of iron and fear that plumed from the timber crate. She licked her ruby lashed lips, eyes darkening beneath their glowing irises. "Final warning, Mr. Townsworth," she growled, trying to leash the thrall bloodlust lashed every vampire with as she observed the decedent toxicity of the girl's lifeblood sliding a tantalising trail, like the sweetest of coulis, down her tenderised porcelain skin. Rounding on him faster than lightning, cane inches from his thick sweat-beading neck she spat. "Experiment on older cattle. It does not bode well for us to deplete the youth of our crop." She whipped around, listening to the fluttering breaths of the child with rapt excitement shining in her eyes before shuttering the longing thrall to bury her fangs inside the succulent flesh down. Taking his kill was beneath her, and yet something about riling this vermin unfit to be given the gift of life hereafter had her quivering with rapt ecstasy. She bared her fangs at him, lowering the shining globe of her cane. "You have until dusk," she proclaimed, her lips pulling back in a toothy smile that highlighted the eerie spectacle of her shining eyes.

"No, no, that is not enough time. I'm close, so close. Give me until dusk tomorrow, a full day," he begged, hurrying after her as she made her way swiftly to the exit, her cane clanking alongside the click of her heels. The old docking yard was full enough to slow her retreat and allow Gilbert to hobble after her without losing her from his sight. Panting he slowed to a stop, leaning heavily against one crate. The vampiress sure could move and the tricky wench had tried to lose him amongst the timber crates by circling a few before her untimely exit. Although, she could have been collecting evidence on the current situation of the herd and the stock of them he held. It was uncanny of her, but Gilbert suspected that it was the case, as the Council had procured the shipping dock in the first place, through an array of unsightly transactions with the former owners.

"Unacceptable, Mr. Townsworth. The Council has decided. It is time to put an end to these pointless experiments of yours. Dusk. That is final!" she snapped, the receding clink of her heeled shoes pinpointing the crest of waves that lapped at the harbour as she slammed her cane down hard on the cobblestones and vanished.

Gilbert's fangs had receded with the submission of a lesser vampire in the presence of one more dominant.

His lips curled as she vanished from sight among the crates blocking those nosy enough to pry, and as for errant children who wished to trespass, well, they would become his next victims and deservedly so, re-puncturing his swollen gums with bloody accents.

As if the presence of the Mistress of the Council wasn't enough to leach every bite of happiness he had claimed from the child, the globe of his cane began to glow and whirl. It revealed the beauty of his beloved daughter and the knowledge that the news of no further progress he would have to bestow.

"Father, how much longer?" She pouted through lips as red as roses, her stardust-rimmed eyes glowing in ethereal beauty.

"Daughter, patience, please." He traced the image of her slender cheek with a singular finger, its quick rimmed in congealed blood.

"Look, father," she said with a glimmering smile, standing to twirl in her room, lifting her skirts to reveal the beautiful blood-stained slippers he had gifted her. "They're perfect, are they not?" She spun once more before falling to the floor in a parachute of skirts flailing around her, hands clasping her face, deep heaving sobs wrenching her fine boned frame. "Oh, father, the party is but a few eves away," she mewed.

"Yes, yes, I know," he hurried, tipping his hat to scratch at his bald head.

"Everyone else has their outfits complete," she sniffled, releasing her hands to reveal huge watering eyes.

"Lamia, your dress is beautiful. You're the stardust in my eyes, you know you are. But this project has to be cleared up; the Council—"

The girl in the globe threw her hands back over her face, her frame bowing to her lap as she rocked and sobbed. "The Council? The Council ruins everything!"

"Hush, hush now, my sweet. All will work out, I promise. It may just take a little more time before I can set up again, somewhere new, and then I will give you every fragrance your heart desires."

"Time! Time!" she screamed, appearing in a fury before the globe's surface. "You promised me a perfume that would make the other vampiresses at the coming-of-age ball fit with a rage of jealousy! You swore to me I would be the most desired at the vampire ball! You're a liar!" she screamed, tears of blood staining tracks down her pale skin.

"My sweet, ple—"

"Liar!"

"Precious, you have to calm dow—"

"Liar! You're no father of mine!" The stardust of her eyes shone blindingly bright as inside the globe the surface on the other side cracked with the force of her slapped strike, only a few broken words seeping through. "—if you loved me—"

Gilbert slammed his cane down hard and the globe on top exploded with the torrent of pressure on both sides of its teleporting screen system. Ripping the top hat from his head and throwing it into the distance didn't release much of his pent-up anger. Nothing ever did, nothing except—

His grin widened. His daughter would have her heart's desire or he would have the heart of Athos's daughter.

***

With all of her screaming, Sally Ann had almost wrought her throat of sound, but when she heard the voice outside of her prison, she began to call like a sorrowful bird chirping for help into an oncoming storm.

She could feel the crust of salt from her tears crystalise as she strained to call for the stranger's aid. But all too soon, her voice rasped its last note, and she lay staring at

Peaches, the human-footed bear, still unable to tackle the sight of her own wound.

She had no idea of the time she had spent in this orchestrated cell. Even so, she was grateful for the frozen water that had awoken her, if only to stave off the stench of her own bodily excretions mixed with the coagulated rust of blood.

The vibrations reverberated around the wooden prison crate holding her, knocking Peaches to her side so they were face to face.

Clunk.

She held her breath to hear it clearer.

Clunk.

It was closer now, so she tried focusing her eyes in the light from the mouth of the crate.

Crack!

Something thick and hard hit her leg just above the oozing flesh of her severed foot. She screamed, but there was no sound left. The gasp of air retracted from her lungs with the burning sting and the amputation's pain awakened. A thick sweat seeped from her brow, her hair clumping to her cheeks as she lurched upright, wrenching her shoulder that popped with relief of its burden, lightening her sorrows by the faintest of touches.

When the black spots cleared from her eyes and the buzz of noise quieted inside her mind, she was staring at the maniac as he crouched, putting them face to grizzly face. "Don't ever try that again," he whispered, "or I will make your stay here so far feel like a stay at the Westminster Palace Hotel. Understand, child?"

Sally Ann nodded, her tremors starting anew. "Good. Now that is agreed upon let's see what we have, shall we?" She watched as his lips curled, his tongue snaking to trace fangs he kept hidden. She could see now in the light of the moon shining clear in its waxing through the open crate. His knobbled hands lay down the cracked cane to go in search of something small hidden in the depths of his blazer's coat pocket.

If I could just reach that cane, she thought, *maybe I could get free. Maybe Peaches and I could escape and find Papa.* But try as she might, her body would barely obey an order her mind fed it. She was starving, thirsty beyond imagination; even after her tongue had lashed every drop of water it was able to, from her rude awakening. To top it all off, she was in agony.

From the trenches of his pockets, he pulled a small glass ampoule, popped the cork from its seal, and held it to her throbbing forehead, collecting every drop of agonising sweat her body created. Sally Ann was stunned into silence; she didn't know what he was doing or what he was looking for. A clink sounded. The maniac's forehead creased as he swirled the liquid, sniffing deeply and sighing. "The fragrance is compelling," he purred, "but it lacks depth." He dropped the ampoule. The mixture inside spread in a thick lumpy goo amongst the smash of glass shards. Sally Ann's vision blurred with the sudden snap of her fingers as one by one, the pressure of his hand cracked them like twigs. The fingers of her left hand wobbled like the broken strings of a puppet and nausea shook her.

***

Gilbert had always been attentive to the matters at hand, especially when involving his daughter's happiness, but he could also get so caught up, that he didn't notice the obvious until it smacked him upside his good arm. He cursed, looking down at an impaling wooden shaft through the blade of his right shoulder. His skin bubbled and hissed with the effects of Holy water the arrow was undoubtedly laced with.

He turned, agony dripping like lust in the heat of battle as he switched on his drill prostatic, pivoting to hunt down his adversary. Sally Ann was left trembling in a half-conscious state with the wide-open crate and the maniac's broken cane lying forgotten next to the unsatisfactory ampoule of human fear.

"As-o-th!" Gilbert purred, wincing every time he lurched forwards. "Come to play, have you?"

"Gilbert, you sick bastard, I'm going to stick your head on a spike for what you've done!" roared the child's kin, a fire's promise of cleansing burning savagely in his aquamarine eyes.

"And what is it that you accuse me of, dearest Asoth?" Gilbert purred.

"You killed my daughter, you psychopathic demon spawn! You will rot in Hell this day!" he bellowed, lifting the already bolted crossbow in his arm. A sharpened bolt of wood smashed like lightning into the shipping crate, which exploded in a bomb of splinters. Gilbert stood, and in a stumbling flash, he moved, hobbling ten times faster than any mortal could in the direction the bolt had originated from.

Gilbert followed the ripple of air left in the bolt's wake just as another shot off, crossing his current path just seconds before impacting his body. His fangs stretched painfully to their limits as he wove around a corner, leaping into the air and rolling onto the top of a hard shipping crate with less sound than a ballerina on pointe. Silkily, he slipped up behind Athos, grabbing his shirt collar to impale his fangs in the supple neck of his nemesis. Athos spun, his crossbow smashing across Gilbert's face, wrenching the vampire's jaw sideways and batting him back with the impact.

Before he could stabilise his motions, Athos slammed his foot into the centre of his back, toppling him from the crate with a crunch no mere mortal would survive.

Pain ripped up his spine. His hobbled leg already ached with the memory of his last encounter with Athos. The human had gotten the upper hand and sloshed Holy water over his leg until it singed and burnt, bubbling away to a hobbled state of grotesque shining skin suctioned to his very bones. Wooden stake and Holy water wounds never healed, and neither did a cross if it touched an immortal's skin; it would burn and then scar for eternity. But this time, Athos would suffer, and he knew exactly how.

"Athos Gabriel Helsing, I pity you," he purred, rising unsteadily from the cobbled ground, the plasma of his sire leaking in rivulets from his partially caved-in skull. It would heal soon; with his vampiric heritage came great strength and restoration, all apart from the injuries and ailments sustained before vampirism.

"Says the monster born of blood," Athos spat, taking aim from the top of the wooden shipping crate again. "I will see your demise, demon!"

"Aah," he licked a lengthened fang, "but not today—" he chuckled wetly. He could feel his eyes brighten, his skull reflate, and his spine straighten as his heritage fixed his ailments. He did not move as Athos sighted down the crossbow. He didn't even pretend to breathe, just snarled a smile he knew would shake the very core of the man's heart with fear, flicking his eyes to the open crate, wherein the child groaned.

"Oh God," were the last words he heard before slipping into his renewed strength and speed with ease and hobbling faster than any human could hope to run. When he entered the shipping crate, his grin stretched his face tight; he hadn't been this happy for centuries. Today, he would put an end to Athos G. Helsing for good. But first, he would make him suffer for hobbling his leg, for haunting his very existence; it was finally time that Athos paid.

***

Sally Ann could hear him, although she was unsure if she was amid a hallucination again.

But she had to try, had to somehow gain his attention; just in case it really was Papa, in case he had come to save her.

Blood loss was becoming a problem, but with adrenaline coursing through her veins, Sally Ann pulled and dragged her broken body with her singular good arm closer to the entrance. But all too soon, dark spots of pain polka-dotted her vision. Her mind spun, ears ringing, no longer able to hear what was going on outside of the crate. Groaning her agony into the air, she prayed the slight breeze would carry her plea before everything turned black.

***

Pain. Red-hot and searing. Her nerves were raw to the elements and the coarse unsanded wood grain abraded her tortured body as it was dragged back inside the quarantine of the crate. She fell upright—crack! Her head hit something hard and blackness engulfed her again.

***

Sally Ann heard the wet chuckles of her tormentor before opening her eyes, their energy lacking so that she could only gaze through the cage of her dark lashes as the maniac ripped into Peaches' arm with those gigantic fangs and spat it out. He grinned menacingly at her, placing the one-armed bear beside her.

The intervals between her consciousness were depleting now and every waking moment appeared stunted like an old black and white film that's slides had become stuck. She was no longer afraid, just glad that the end of her suffering was in sight—that she could die and at last, be at peace. Or so she thought.

***

She regained consciousness for what she thought was the final time, as before her, the maniac switched the button that had his drill appendage thrumming. Suddenly he was on his knees before her, licking at his swollen lips. Then everything went white. The cold bite of savage metal churned as he thrust the drill towards Sally Ann's heart.

***

"Sire be damned!" Gilbert roared as lifeblood pooled into impressionism of J.M.W Turner's oil paintings around him. His prosthetic drill was suctioned tight into the chest cavity now and it took a slurping pop for him to pull it free and cease its tearing momentum. Sweat pooled on his furrowed brow as he glared down at the blood-soaked body of his interfering arch-nemesis, Asoth. The bastard had flung himself before the child and his drill had greedily accepted his sacrifice.

Gilbert lurched back, slamming his hand down to support his frame and cursing when it cut on the shards of ampoule he had discarded earlier. But he barely felt the bite of glass puncture his skin as anger rolled like a tsunami through his plasma stream. His prostatic drill shook, splatters dropping from his arm as he narrowed his vision down upon the child, his ears reverberating with the ringing of her screams as she fell over her father, Asoth's body, crying.

Then, just as a smile split his face, another sound caught his attention, a click of the main door, and Gilbert swore, snatched up his smashed cane, and slammed it into the side of the crate. "I was so close, so close," he raged, ripping the girl from her father and clenching her jawbone in his hand, disabling her mouth to stop her wailing. Gilbert had thought the child would be all out of tears, he thought he had made her incapable of any more emotion. He had imagined that by now she would be lost to pain and misery, but this, this was so much more. He could feel his eyes glowing with excitement. His fangs throbbing with blood lust. And then, he saw it: a glimmer of bloody sweat from her body, the teardrop of terror he had promised his daughter as a gift to celebrate her coming of age.

"Mr. Townsworth, it is time!"

"Mistress," he hissed, his eyes never leaving the drops of terror he had finally procured from the young human. He watched as every pore in the child's body wept, the thick tang of iron scented the air as droplets of bloody sweat seeped through her skin like diamonds surfacing from a sinkhole.

Releasing the child's pinched-in jaw and leaving deep scratches in his wake, he quickly searched his coat pocket for another ampoule, pressed it to the child's skin, and collected a gift worth more than gold.

He held it up before him, marvelling at the beauty, the intoxicating aroma disabling him. Suddenly the ampoule was snatched from his hand. Gilbert spun on his knees, rising to attack the thief but then: crack! The last sound he heard was his neck snapping in one quick, lethal swipe as her cane connected with his undead flesh.

***

Sally Ann blinked. Her eyes prickled their displeasure at opening their rejuvenated nerve system. Her squinting gaze hunted for her papa, desperate to prove the nightmare of earlier wrong. But although his weight no longer lay lifeless across her lap, she couldn't help but let her gaze travel the slick trail to her papa's remains dumped in a corner of the crate, the tell-tale strap of his boot buckle. She tilted her head slightly to one side, expecting even in her youth for the shredding heartbreak of her loss to affect her more than just the few minutes before she blacked out. Her brow furrowed as she cocked her head to the opposite side and tried to move her fingers. Her right side complied, although a deep throb resonated through them, the digits of her left hand hung limp like severed strings, numb like her heart.

A short stumpy woman stood in heels before her, one arm out, indicating the maniac. He lay in a crumpled mess of limbs at her feet. His head was bent at a strange angle. Sally Ann gazed at him with renewed sight. She felt the pressure inside her bubbling as the woman ordered the maniac's permanent elimination. Sally Ann watched as a young man, maybe five years her senior, pulled the stake her papa had shot through Gilbert's shoulder free and slammed it into the monster's demonic heat.

Suddenly Sally Ann erupted in hiccupping chuckles like she had when she sat down for tea with Peaches in the garden—that had felt so long ago. Her heart squeezed tightly as convulsions took her body and a set of stardust-rimmed eyes compelled her from death into her new life.

PART 3

Sally Ann stood no taller than her eight-year-old self and not a day physically older. But her mind had aged in smarts and cunning. She wore an ice blue dress with a large silk bow tied at the waist. She hummed contentedly to herself, waiting. She had spent twenty years at the vampire finishing school, learning to adapt to her new life, to hunt, and to survive.

The Council had sent her there, where twenty years of training would feel like a lifetime to a human, but it was a mere breath in the life of a vampire. The Council at first had considered her destruction, due to her birth into their world being of such a horrific nature. But after losing Gilbert Townsworth, her jailer and torturer, they found out that he had not only procured an ampoule of terror, a fragrance so rare and sought after that only the Queen of their race could afford. But that he had also accidentally sired her through the ingestion of his plasma into her bloodstream via the mere scrap of glass that had bloodied his hand.

It had only been when Mistress Beatrice stepped in saying that they as a Council owed the clan for the loss of such scientific talent and knowledge that they agreed there might be a small chance that she would inherit some ability bestowed by her unintentional sire. And that said ability might just come in handy for the future of the clan. So they let her live, hoping every day for an ability that did not bloom. Many hypothesized the theory that her 'awakening' was too traumatic. Others merely chose to nip and threaten the ability out of her—for the good of the clan—her classmates would hiss. But, Sally Ann got through their judgements and their ire. But never had she been able to wipe away the assault of congealing plasma so bitter it rivalled any acidic fruit as it rolled onto her tongue and down her young human throat.

The gruesome drops she had ingested from her 'sire' had her gagging at the thought even today. Yet every vampire present in the line-up, of those coming of age, had described their sire's blood as ambrosia. Everyone except her. Sally Ann had spent years under the oppression of the Council, years plotting and planning for this very day, this very moment. She smiled as the vampire before her was called to present, received his cane then flicked her a subtle wink. She smiled back, a twisted kind of smile that left the receiver wondering if she truly knew the meaning of it or not.

Finally. it was her turn to be presented at the coming-of-age ball.

She stepped forward among the throng of vampires.

"—and finally, may I present Sally Ann," announced Mistress Beatrice.

"And Peaches," she corrected with a low curtsy. Peaches' paw held tightly in one hand, its other still missing, just the ragged stitch of a child keeping it together. Its heart no longer glowed and its fur was musty and old with the scent of iron from the stapled decomposing limb of her human foot. She missed it even now, but she could manage quite well with the splinted over-knee boots laced up, and anyway, Peaches needed it more.

"Congratulations dear," Mistress Beatrice cooed, reaching a hand out towards the rack of canes, a vampire's rite of passage into society and their primary means of communication, awaiting her assistant to hand her one. "—and what dream do you have to go out into the world with, my dear?" the stout vampiress with gleaming fangs framing her ruby red lips inquired. She waited for an answer with a slight tilt to her head, her ceremonial cane standing higher than most attendees, even putting those of the other Council members to shame with its sceptre's appearance. In all the long, gruesome years she had been forced into attending this academy Sally Ann had dreamt of her 'awakening' into the undead every-single-night. She had smelt the iron taint of her own life blood and too her repulsion, she now felt thirst. A thirst that mingled with horrors now living, with monsters calling her—the daughter of Asoth Gabriel Helsing—friend.

A throat cleared, jolting her thoughts and Sally Ann rose, turning to face Mistress Beatrice, ignoring the crowd. "I'm going to get Peaches a new heart."

Mistress Beatrice chuckled. "Then you will be needing this." She twitched her fingers in agitation at her assistant's slothly speed, sparing a quick glance at the vampire who aimlessly fumbled to release a shiny red cane with a globe mechanism polished to a twinkle. But as his hand gripped the cane Mistress Beatrice snapped her fingers. Pointed to a cane tucked in the back of the stand where it stood sentry over the mass, disregarded, but ever watchful. It was a decrepit looking cane, the bulbous globe smooth, even though the echo of a scar smashed into it still lay visible.

Sally Ann frowned at it in confusion, tracing its scar with the subtle fingers of her mind. Her eyes sparked suddenly, a twisted smile alighting her childish face as the vampire assistant handed it to the Mistress.

"I'm sure you will remember this," she purred, her own eyes alighting with the lure of a hunt, the thrall of blood lust. Her smile was that of nightmares, like the jack-in-a-box clown that wavered menacingly to and fro on its spring, lips of swollen red on its crafted face, its teeth a nightgown white.

Sally Ann greedily snatched it from her offering hand, a thrill like no other raced through every fiber of her being. This was it. This was the time she had been waiting for, the precipice of her new, undead existence. She turned to the staff, flicking a switch that caused the mechanism that dialed any vampire the user had a connection to. She thought of the voice she heard whining for the ampoule as she suffered unimaginable torture. The globe began to swirl with smoke as it opened its call to stardust-rimmed eyes. Sally Ann felt her smile spread, the tender ache in her face a delicacy as she tilted her head to one side, winked, and waved Peaches' paw at the girl in the crystal. Smiling, eyes wide and glistening, she sang her message into the globe.

"I'm coming."

BIOGRAPHY & THANKS

A bit about me (OMG — skip this bit quickly!).

Okay, if you're still checking this out then you want to know something new, so here goes: this is my very first fantasy horror, vampire story and traditionally published manuscript.

Wow, right? As I generally write dark fantasy, I was excited to challenge myself with something new and darker.

I wrote this novella in my family's country cottage (that's where we live—I'm not rich lol) situated next to a graveyard. (I thought you would like that juicy fact.)

I've always dreamt of becoming a fully-fledged authoress. So I have a lot of people who have helped me on my journey so far:

A big thank you to Dean of DEMAIN Publishing for believing in this novella and giving me my first big break.

Thank you to Dave Jeffery who helped me see clearly, pointed me at a target and wrote his awesome cover quote for me.

Thank you to Adrian for this awesome cover design; Roberto for his artwork and Tia for being a brilliant model.

Thank you to 'Monkeys With Typewriters' who allowed me to be a part of their group during lockdown.

Thank you to all of you who have helped, guided or been there for me.

And last but never least thank you Reader for checking out this heinous tale and coming on a horrific adventure with me.

Hearts & Kisses

Carrie Weston, August 2022

DEMAIN PUBLISHING

To keep up to-date on all news DEMAIN (including future submission calls and releases) you can follow us in a number of ways:

BLOG:
www.demainpublishingblog.weebly.com

TWITTER:
@DemainPubUk

FACEBOOK PAGE:
Demain Publishing

INSTAGRAM:
demainpublishing

Printed in Great Britain
by Amazon